Phillips Brooks

Inspiration and Truth

Phillips Brooks

Inspiration and Truth

ISBN/EAN: 9783337184032

Printed in Europe, USA, Canada, Australia, Japan

Cover: Foto ©Andreas Hilbeck / pixelio.de

More available books at **www.hansebooks.com**

INSPIRATION AND TRUTH

FROM THE RIGHT REV-
EREND PHILLIPS BROOKS
DOCTOR OF DIVINITY AND
BISHOP OF MASSACHUSETTS

BOSTON
J. G. CUPPLES COMPANY
THE BACK BAY BOOK STORE
250 BOYLSTON STREET

CONTENTS.

Education.

THE true future does not repeat but enlarges the present. And every present which accepts this law accepts with it its appointed work, to gather the stones and the timbers for the temples which the future is to build. It makes this the principle on which it proceeds in training a new generation. It disciplines the child with reverence, as destined to a completer life than the parent. It transcends selfishness, and prejudice, and jealousy, and, with a large and loving hope, a complete faith in human progress, it imagines no perfection for itself except this relative one of perfectly filling its place in the gradual perfection of the whole.

YOU will see how this truth, which makes the teacher in this great world-school always recognize that the scholar is to have larger work than his to do, will make all education of necessity a profound and thorough thing. It insists on teaching principles and truths, and is not satisfied with just imposing forms.

WE look back over history, and we see the same sight always. Wherever any age has given its successor nothing but forms and institutions ready-made, the new age has not merely made no advance upon the old; it has invariably shrunk and shriveled till it lived a life too small even to fill the narrow limits which its father claimed. But wherever any age has given its child an education in any vital truths, the child has always taken those truths, developed them into an effectiveness and built them into a beauty that the father never guessed.

THE Jew was so used to the sublime thought of human life held fast in the hands of the Divine authority, shaped into gradual rectitude by the continual pressure of command and prohibition; the decalogue so supremely represented to him the first thought of religion, that his prayer for a new generation's religious life touched of necessity first of all upon the moral side, the keeping of the commandments of the Lord. And here, I take it, the Jew simply conceives the course of all successful culture.

THE order of the Testaments is not an accidental, but an essential order. Calvary, in its idea, in its divine conception was "from the foundation," long before Sinai; but in man's apprehension of them, Sinai antedated Calvary by fifteen hundred years. The conscience must bow itself to the supreme "Thou shalt" and "Thou shalt not" of authority, before grace can enter in to win the heart with the gentle persuasiveness of its "Believe and live." John the Baptist must preach repentance before Christ can proclaim regeneration.

GOD wastes no history. In every age and every land He is working for the elucidation of some moral truth, some riper culture for the character of man.

The State.

GOVERNMENT is an incorporated, an embodied truth. Get any high idea about it, get beyond the thought that a nation is just a multitude of men who have happened to come together in a certain country, and who have bargained among themselves not to hurt each other, not to rob and kill each other, and you must come to this, that every nation is a divine utterance before the world of certain principles, of providence, of brotherhood, of justice, of the divine and human lives. The highest conception of the state, as of the world, is that it is an uttered thought of God, a certain colossal utterance of truth.

THE healthy state, like the healthy human body, can tolerate nothing within it that will not become part and parcel of itself, ready to share its fortunes, ready to do its work. A scholarship which tries to live in the state and yet not be of it, setting itself apart, fastidious, critical, captious, however thorough or elegant it may be, is mischievous. The politician who lives the life to which all politicians tend, of isolation from the common public interests, thinking that the state and government are things for him to use, and not that he is their instrument; that they exist for him, not he for them,—he is a terrible curse always. May God rid us of him speedily.

A GREAT public life moving healthily

will warn us of any coming dangers, as the ocean itself rings the storm-bell that tells of its own tumults.

THE time has . . . passed when a Sunday-school book need count it unworthy of its pages to help some boy in the city or on the prairies to gather up, with the love of the Lord who is to save him, a love of the land he may be called to die for, and of all the great race to which, if he lives at all worthily, his life is to be given.

I PLEAD with you for all that makes strong citizens. First, clear convictions, deep, careful, patient study of the government under which we live, until you not merely believe it is the best in all

the world, but know why you believe.
And then a clear conscience, as clear in
private interests, as much ashamed of
public as of private sin, as ready to hate
and rebuke and vote down corruption in
the state, in your own party, as you
would be in your own store or church ;
as ready to bring the one as the other
to the judgment of a living God.   And
then unselfishness : an earnest and ex-
alted sense that you are for the land,
and not alone the land for you ; something of the self-sacrifice which they
showed who died for us from '61 to '65.
And then activity : the readiness to wake
and watch and do a citizen's work un-
tiringly, counting it as base not to vote
at an election, not to work against a bad
official, or to work for a good one, as it
would have been to shirk a battle in the
war.   Such strong citizenship let there

be among us; such knightly doing of
our duties on the field of peace.

A STATE is not merely an idea, or an
accident, or a machine, but is a being
with the privilege of force.

SOMEWHERE, sometimes, it will assert
itself strongly in the action of the world.
Busied mostly within itself, in its own
self-regulation, in the development of
its own resources, and in the extension
of its influence through the peaceful
machineries of commerce and negotia-
tion, there must be in it a power to
enforce itself at the call of justice upon
the unwilling action either of its own

subjects who separate themselves in rebellion from it, or against other nations who wantonly set themselves in the way of its just growth.

SINCE truth lives in outward structures, and embodies itself in governments, it has not merely its spiritual relations to wills, but its physical relations to actions. It is hindered not only by unconverted hearts, but by armed rebellions. And so it has a right and need to say not merely to the will "Believe," but to the action "Submit." It has not merely its higher functions of *persuasion*, but its lower functions, too, of *force*.

War.

H, how alike all history seems! How old, and yet eternally how new, these elementary emotions are! How the first instincts that make men fight for freedom, and good government, and truth, last on from age to age! old and yet ever young, like the eternal skies, the ever self-renewing trees, the gray and child-like sea!

DISPERSING armies and hanging traitors, imperatively as justice and necessity may demand them both, are not the killing of the spirit out of which they sprang.

IT is not the least of the debts that we owe to our Union soldiers that their very graves are vocal—that though dead they speak to us still.

THE men who from the bloody shore of the Rebellion embarked into the other life have left their foot-prints inefface-able upon the margin where they planted them, and made it recognizable and dear forever.

IT is because in them, in what they were and what they did, the best of our national character shone out, that these soldiers have won a dearness and a permanent memory that do not belong merely to their personality. The nation honors in them its truest representatives. The real life of the land sees in them the ideal life which is the true outcome of its institutions. They were the flower of its principles, and so it sprinkles its memorial flowers on their graves.

It was a noble gift of Providence that in one man [Washington] should be comprised and pictured, for the dullest eyes to see, the majesty and meaning of the struggle that gave our nation birth.

Oh, the mysterious power of a death for a noble cause! The life is truly given. It passes out of the dying body into the cause, which lives anew.

When the great ship had hardly rounded into port; while, standing on the shore of peace, we felt the solid earth still rocking under our feet with the remembered heaving of the sea, they who had watched and labored for her safety through the nights and storms out on mid-ocean, one by one, as if their work was done, began to pass to their reward, and to what other tasks we cannot know, awaiting them in other worlds. What have they left behind them, they and the humbler dead whom votive monuments and tender hearts remember still in every town and hamlet of their land? Not only what they did, not only even what they were, but new tasks like their own for us who stay behind them. They did not merely clear the field of treason. By the same labor they built up a new possibility of national character and life.

They were like the men who, in these stony pastures of Andover, clear the rough field of stones and build the gray wall that is to surround and shelter it, out of the same material, at the same time. . . . . By purer social life, by finer aspirations, by more unselfishness, by heartier hatred of corruption, let us be worthy of them, and in our quiet duties build the true memorial to the characters of those who found their duty in the camp, the prison and the field, and where they found it did it even to the death. They saw that their country was like a precious vase of rarest porcelain, price-less while it was whole, valueless if it was broken into fragments. What they died to keep whole, may we in our seve-ral places live to keep holy! So may we be worthy of them.

As the merchant, the scholar, the statesman, the diplomatist represent the other elements of power in the state, by which she impresses her will upon other wills; so the soldier represents the element of force by which she must be ready to rule action without ruling will when the clear need shall come.

A MERCIFUL Providence kept our first history from becoming a military history. And if we ask how Providence did this good work for us, the answer can be only in the way in which God made the thought and the devotion of the time so strong that force was always kept in its true place, — their servant.

His [the Puritan soldier's] was the great, homely, intelligible utterance of strength, ringing out clear and sharp in the midst of the often thin and over-subtle theologizings of the time, as the dazzling and bewildered atmosphere compresses and discharges its electricity in the piercing lightning and the pealing thunder.

When we look at Washington, we are at once struck by seeing how in him, who represented as a military man the force of the new ideas which were at work, we have also as a thinker, as a statesman and political philosopher, the clearest example of the reason of which that force was the expression. Often the two are disunited. One man does the thinking, another man does the fighting. One man develops the idea in the closet, and another makes it forcible upon the field. Rarely have the two so met in one man. Washington was at once the clearest thinker and the most effective soldier of our Revolutionary struggle.

NEVER was there a fighting-man with less of the purely military passion. He was the armed citizen, armed for a cause that belonged to the very essence of his citizenship. When that cause had triumphed on the field of battle, he laid down his arms and was the unarmed citizen,—the citizen, the same man still contending for precisely the same cause on the field of statesmanlike debate for which he had fought at Trenton and suffered at Valley Forge.

TRUTH in her armor is apt to be a very clumsy giant. Men will forget or deny what must be our belief all through, that the divine mission of force implies that force has no mission save for divine tasks, none for the mere brutalities of selfishness, or ambition, or jealousy, or worldly rage; none for the mere punctilios of national dignity.

FORCE has no right here in the world except as it is simply truth in armor.

THE presence of the distinct military element, the ruler of, or the slave of, but not a part of the nation, not bound up in the nation's fortune, nor sharing the nation's feeling, not springing from the nation's heart, this is what has made the weakness, and at last brought the death of many a noble nation, both of the old and of the modern times. May God save us from it forever.

IT is not necessary to excuse all our people's early or later treatment of the Indian.   From earliest to latest — from the Pilgrim times down to the Indian policies of these last days—there is too much that never can be excused.

WE are suffering to-day [June 5, 1864], whatever be the secondary causes, for the violation of two of God's great moral laws, the law of the sacredness of government and the law of the brotherhood of man. Gradually, grandly, from between these fearful wheels that drip with blood, are being ground forth into shapes which men's eyes, quick-sighted with anxiety, must see, these two eternal ordinances of God, that government has a divine right to be honored, and that man has a divine right to be free. Those two truths, burned into the very fibre of our people as they walk the fire, are to be the great moral acquisition of American character.

Is there one of us that can look about him and think without a shudder of another generation of our people working out this same education that we are going through? What! all these fearful years again? Again these battles that the eye cannot count or the heart remember? Again this waste of precious blood, this bitter hatred, these wild blazings-up of the devilish in man, this land with State on State where the harvests find no room to grow for the crowded graves? Must it all come again, this dark Egyptian Passover-night of history, wherein God leads the bondmen out, and, in all the stricken land that held them slaves, leaves in their deliverance "not a house where there is not one dead"? We have no right to leave a chance behind us that this work will have to be done again. But it must be, unless we can bring out of it all, clearly and definitely and forever settled, and lay down before the next age of Americans, the truths of national authority and human liberty, to be the materials out of which it is to build the future.

A TRUTH starts on its way across the world, sent by God to possess the world; and that truth meets its obstacles,— obstinate and resisting men. It lays itself against the wills of those men. By every method of approach, through the affections and the conscience and the sense of beauty, and in every other way, it tries to get power over those wills and make them yield to it. It tries to rule the will and so to reach the actions which will be spontaneously obedient when the will has once submitted. It largely succeeds. That is the success it most desires. But when its efforts of persuasion and conviction have failed to remove any one obstinate enemy out of its path, what then? Surely, unless physical force be of a wholly immoral nature, we must believe that God has so arranged his universe that this beleaguered and hindered truth may claim the powers that can compel the action even when they cannot turn the will, and force out of its way an enemy who will not turn into a friend.

The Church.

LO ! it dawns upon you that the Church is not to be made, that the Church is here already. In the aggregate of all this Christly life you have the Church of Christ, just as truly as in the aggregate of human existence you have humanity. One has no more to be made than the other. Both exist in their components.

THE Romish idea is that the Church thinks and struggles and receives help and revelation. The Protestant idea is that thought and struggle and help and light come to the Man.

THE living souls must go before the living Church, which has no life except in them. . . . Churches live in their souls. O, the old struggles, so endless and so fruitless, that history has to show, of men and times that tried to keep a Church alive without caring for the life of souls; men and times which seem to have strangely fancied that there was a certain power of vitality in the very Church itself, so that every soul on earth might cease to receive inflow of Christ and yet somehow the Church live on! It is the danger of the ecclesiastical spirit. It is the danger for all Churchmen and all Church times to fear.

THE Church, whose purpose in being is merely to feed her children's life and so increase her own, may harm the very life that she was meant to cultivate. This is nothing strange. Nothing is so likely to stop a stream of water as the broken or displaced fragments of the very earthen pipe through which it was meant to flow.

IF a Church, in any way, by hindering the free play of human thoughtfulness upon religious things, by clothing with mysterious reverence, and so shutting out from the region of thought and study, acts and truths which can be thoroughly used only as they are growingly understood, by limiting within hard and minute and invariable doctrinal statements the variety of the relations of the human experience to God, if, in any such way, a Church hinders at all the free inflow of every new light which God is waiting to give to the souls of men as fast as they are ready to receive it, just so far she blinds and wrongs her children's intelligence and weakens her own vitality. This is the suicide of Dogmatism.

IF, again, a Church, in any way, sets any technical command of hers to stand so across the path, that a command of God cannot get free access to the will of any of the least of all God's people; if there be, as there has been again and again, a system of ecclesiastical morality different from the eternal morality which lies above the Church, between the soul and God, a morality which hides some eternal duties and winks at some eternal

sins, just so far as there is any such ob-
liquity turning aside the straight, bright
ray that is darting right from the throne
of the God-soul to the will of the Man-
soul, just so far the Church maims and
wrongs her children's consciences, and
weakens her own vitality. This is the
suicide of Corruption.

AGAIN, if the symbols of the Church,
which ought to convey God's love to
man, become so hard that the love does
not find its way through them, and they
stand as splendid screens between the
Soul and the Love, or have such a pos-
itive character of their own, so far forget
their simple duty of pure transparency
and mere transmission, that they send
the Love down to the Soul colored with

themselves, formalized and artificial; if the Church dares either to limit into certain material channels, or to bind to certain forms of expression, that love of God which is as spiritual and as free as God, then yet again she is false to her duty, she binds and wrongs her children's loving hearts, and once again she weakens her own vitality. This is the suicide of Formalism.

THE time must come when Religion shall no longer make artificial virtues and vices of her own, and when with more unsparing tongue she shall detect and praise or denounce those virtues and vices which are essential and eternally the same. Then a thousand rills of life will be open into her which are closed to-day, and she will live a thousand-fold.

OF the essential life of the Church, of the truly living Church, what can we say but this, that it is that which most completely feels that it was made for men, not men for it; which, therefore, lives only as it lives in them; which strives for nothing but to open more and more the channels of life from Christ to them? In such a church and such a church alone can be real unity. To be full of such a care for, and spirit of servantship to, the human soul, is the only power that can keep our own Church one in the midst of all her distractions. No outer bond of history or government can permanently hold her. Only this common purpose, freely working in the Church at large, can keep the true organic unity of life, which is the only unity worth having. The live pomegranate holds itself together with no

string tied round it. The dead pomegranate cracks and breaks. No tight-
est string can hold it. The Living
Church of truth, obedience, and spiritual
love, will guard its own integrity. The
disintegration of error, corruption or
formalism, what compactest system can
withstand!

THE Church does not become the
world's savior by furnishing it with a
powerful police.

THE true relations between moral law
and religious life are certainly not so
difficult as men have made them. Moral
action is, in one sense, the end; that is,
it is the necessary result of religion, not
its final purpose. In another sense,
moral law is the means by which the

religious impulse steadies and supports itself, and mounts to higher spiritual heights. In this last sense, it is the very highest order of machinery, but it is machinery still. So that even if the Church were, what she has tried to be often, and has sometimes been to some extent, the great Reformer, breaking down sins, turning wrongs into rights, ruling men's actions everywhere; glorious as such a sight would be, it would not be the Church communicating life. She would be purifying and cultivating her own life. She would be making the world ready for the life she had to give it, but not giving it yet.

WONDERFULLY adapted to be the channel of the highest devotion, the deepest utterance of faith, submission and repentance, the very perfect machinery of Christian living, the Church system is dead without some power of Christian life.

So again of every sacred rite which, through the senses, opens a way for power to reach the heart. It is machinery still. The sensuous impression may make the soul receptive, no doubt it does, to some of the more external messages of God. But the impression itself is not soul-life. It is not a new birth, though its frightened or ecstatic shiver is easily enough mistaken for another Genesis.

WHO of us has not seen, nay, who of us in the deader moments of his parish life has not done, Church work enough —Sunday-schools, Bible-classes, night-schools, parish visiting, mothers' meetings and reading-rooms and all that — which he knew was only the mechanical whirling of the spindles by hand, with the vital fires utterly gone out in the furnaces below.

WHAT shall we say of Preaching? Only that if men can preach, and preach the very truth of Christ, year after year, and yet souls, thirsty for the water of life, sit at the dry mouths of their well-built channels and thirst in vain for help and salvation, then it must be that the mere telling the Truth as the mind can understand it and the lips can speak it, is not necessarily the communication of the Gospel Life.

THE Church . . . needs more of the Lord ; more knowledge, more obedience, more love of Jesus Christ. Unless we get that, and make that bear upon men's hearts and souls, we may chant our own sweetest praises in their ears, and our appeal for sympathy will be only very piteous. It will sound to the world as the plaintive cries of the Church do sound to many men under their windows, like the beggar's violin, which neither claims tribute by the right of a governor, nor wins acknowledgment by the skill of an artist, but only extorts charity by the forlornness of the mendicant.

IF behind muscles, and blood, and brain, you know that there is a vital force, which utters itself through them, but which is another thing than they, which would live even if they were dead, then it is not strange to say that behind all morality, and order, and rites, and work, and preaching, there is a vital power of the Church, which utters itself through them, but which is another thing than they, without which they were dead, but which might live though every one of them should die. That life-power is Christ always entering into the Church, as truth, and guidance, and love; and always passing out from the Church into humanity by the otherwise dead functions, vitalized by Him, of teaching and government, and active work.

As in the world of science men fear materialism which would crowd spirit and vital force out of the universe, and make all life exist and spread itself in the mechanical arrangement and re-arrangement of material atoms; so there is always fear, and never more fear than now, of an ecclesiastical materialism, which shall make little of spiritual force, and try by the mechanical arrangement and re-arrangement of ecclesiastical atoms, of dioceses, and conventions, and canons, and rubrics, and the like, to make the dead world live the life of God. Such a materialism turns machineries from being the homes into being the tombs of force, and makes us dread each step we see it take in advance.

IF ever our Church goes back, and cumbers herself with the precedents, and submits herself to the influence or authority, of the English Church, her power in this land is gone. She must be part and parcel of this people. She must be in heart and soul American, or she is nothing. She must have her sympathies here, and not across the sea. She must have her gaze and enthusiasm fixed upon the future of America, and not upon the past of England.

WE can conceive of a parish going on, the same parish still, though thought shall change and all religious speculation flow in new channels. But if men's souls cease to repent, and trust, and live by the divine communion, all is gone; the

Church is dead; the spiritual building crumbles in decay.

I KNOW that you will more than accept under the great, glowing, all-embracing hospitality of this bounteous roof [that of Trinity Church, Boston], you will enthusiastically assert, that such a Church as this has no right to exist, or to think that it exists, for any limited company who own its pews. It would not be a Christian parish if it harbored such a thought. No, let the world come in. Let all men hear, if they will, the truths we love. Let no soul go unsaved through any selfishness of ours.

THIS is the modern notion of a Church, — not luxury, but work.

ANY man or any institution which
attempts a great religious work in behalf
of the growing generations of a country,
must undertake, as preparatory to it, and
as a necessary part of it, a great moral
work as well. A faithful ministry, we
hold, must not merely declare the Savior,
but must attack and beat down those
special sins which stand in the very door-
ways and keep the Savior out of the
hearts of men.

THERE are cases in which the move-
ment of the will is everything; where to
move action without moving will is to
fail entirely. In such cases there can be
no room for force. This is why our
Lord, founding a religion whose whole
life was to be in converted wills, found

no place in its establishment or propaga-
tion for the sword.

THE Church has been spread by force,
but Christianity never.   To try to think
of extending a faith by force, is to try
to think a contradiction.   It is like
thinking of raising enthusiasm with levers,
or crushing genius with sledge-hammers.
The tools have no relation to the material or the task.

I LOOK round on the work to do, and
I do not believe that either Episcopalian-
ism or Methodism or Presbyterianism
or Baptism is going to assert the victory
of Christianity over sin, the opening of
the barred citadel of wickedness in this our

land. The Church of Christ, simple, un-
impeded, armed powerfully because
armed lightly, the essential Church of
Christ must make the first entrance.
Then let us have up our methods of denominational government, and each, in
the way that he thinks most divine, strive
for the perfected dominion of our one
great Lord.

JUST as in God's great sea there is a
tide-power and a wave-power, and both
are the outputtings of the one same
force; just as neither denies the other,
each lends the other impulse; and the
quick waves, which fall like lashes, and
the slow, heaving, laboring tide, have
both their work to do in the eternal battle of the sea upon the land: so it is not
inconceivable that in the Christian world

there may be a church-force and a de-
nomination-force, which yet are both the
expression of one same purpose and de-
sign of Deity.

THE waves that crest themselves with
angry foam, and beat and beat and beat
from sunrise round to sunrise endlessly
upon the stubborn beach, are the most
visible agents of the work that is done.
But who will find anything but thankful-
ness, if once in every world-day the great
hand of the Maker and the Watcher is
put down under the great mass of the
sea itself, and the deep tide of Christian
law and Christian truth, with all the
waves running their eager races on its
bosom, is driven, mightily, silently, far-
ther up than any wave had reached upon
the conquered shore? Who will com-

plain if Christian union, for certain purposes, in certain efforts, develops a new
sort of power that the narrower individu-
ality of denominational life has not at-
tained?

THE everlasting principle remains, that
no moral authority or doctrinal correct-
ness or spiritual impulse can last from
generation to generation unimpaired, unless it incorporates itself in some recog-
nized manifestation, and yields to the
crystallization which its essential life de-
mands.

Scepticism.

HE countless assaults of a speculative time, testing every approach, bringing the manifold artillery of modern knowledge to bear, calling both the frivolity and the earnestness of our strange age to its aid, enlisting an internal treason as well as an external enmity — no wonder that they make the boldest fear sometimes. The rain is descending, the floods are coming, the winds are blowing and beating, and when loose houses are sliding off the slippery sand on every side of them, no wonder that the dwellers in the house upon the rock, with dazzled eyes, think sometimes that they see their own foundation waver. And yet the case does not seem hard to understand.

CHRISTIANITY is one and everlasting. Its work of salvation for man's soul is the same blessed work forever. But its relation to the world's life at large must be forever changing with the changes of that world's needs and seekings. The larger applications of Christianity must of necessity be from time to time readjusted, and in their readjustments its power may be temporarily obscured or unrecognized as it passes into new forms of exhibition. Is it strange, then, in a day of readjustments such as ours, when so many forms are going to pieces, so many old relations broken up and changed for new ones, when so many of the accidents of Christianity are being taken down, that men should be ready enough to think that Christianity itself is worn out and obsolete?

WE feel no doubt of the eternal issue. Our faith in Christ comes not from seeing how men treat Him, but from reading what God says of Him and feeling how He works. We are sure of the end; that all this overturning, overturning, overturning, must bring at last the day of Him whose right it is.

MEANWHILE, what can we do but keep alive by earnest and continual

utterance those truths which we believe,
no matter how utterly men may disown
their names, are doing the work of the
world all the while? This is one of the
great values of such a time, that it sifts
and ordinates truths, and makes us find
out which are the few precious ones
that we will not let go at any risk.

AND when we look about and ask,
How can we best preserve these truths?
I think there can be but one answer.
The highest truth has always found its
own best guardians. Christ Himself
pointed to the younger generation that
was growing up about Him, and declared
its hands to be the place where His gospel would be safest, purest and most
fruitful. Other years have their work to

do — old age, and middle manhood, and the fresh enterprise of originating youth. But, after all, these are not the surest guardians of truth.

THROUGH the life of every people winds an endless procession, which appears to totter with its feebleness, which again and again is lost out of sight among the hurrying crowd that seems to tread it under foot, and yet whose tiny hands bear safest and most pure forever the sacred treasures of all time. And if you once get a truth into the circle of that endless childhood, it makes its way to unfound hearts, and, through the crazy passions and cold bigotries of life, wins for itself an influence which men feel because they do not fear.

IT was not far from the time when this Church [Trinity Church, Boston] was founded, that Bishop Butler wrote in England words which seem strange, I think, to us as we read them now. He said, "It has come to be taken for granted, by many persons, that Christianity is not so much a matter of inquiry, but that it is now at length discovered to be fictitious." And, after all that, see what life came out of what men called dead. A great many people are saying now what people used to say in Bishop Butler's day, but it is no truer now than it was then.

Life.

THERE are two souls in the world, the soul of God and the soul of man; no other. .... The God-soul is the centre of all things. The souls of men stand around and gather all their culture and their growth from it.

No enumeration of qualities or faculties of matter accounts to us for physical vitality; and no description of man taught and ruled and loved by God, makes clear to us that life of God imparted to man which we call holiness. Only this we are sure of, that all Spiritual Life, whether in these its elements, or in this subtle force which blends the elements into a true vitality, is an inflow from the soul of God into the soul of Man.

LIFE can only be truly communicated by truly living methods.   Nothing else will do.   This takes all power away from mere machineries from the highest to the lowest.

THAT is what we want,— strong, deep convictions which are unshakable, and then a glad and constant expectation of new and richer light from God forever; a perfect assurance of the safety of the ship in which we sail, and then a perfect willingness to sail into whatever new seas

God may open to us; an absolute cer-
tainty of the sufficiency of Christ, and
then a passionate desire that no Christ
of our own fancy may satisfy us, that He
may show Himself to us more and more
completely as He really is; the rock under our feet and the limitless air over our
heads.

THROUGH our fathers' wisdom and
devotion, we must become wiser and
more devoted than they. Friends, we
must rise to thoughts beyond our fathers,
or we are not our fathers' worthy children. Not to do in our days just what
our fathers did long ago, but to live as
truly up to our light as our fathers lived
up to theirs, — that is what it is to be
worthy of our fathers.

THOSE be our prayers:—More strength; more light. More constancy; more progress.

THE man of the nineteenth century thinks very differently from the man of the eighteenth, but the love with which he worships God, is the same love. The Evangelical has different dogmas from the old Georgian Churchman, but they bow before the same mercy-seat, and resist the same temptations by the same grace.

A MAN is always more precious than his work.

EVERYWHERE, always, good culture

and the championship of principles belong together.

THAT men should be true to their best
convictions, and to their simple duty,
this is the blessing that gives all bless-
ings with it, and is the fountain of all
charity and progress.

IT is Truth that we want in every de-
partment of our life. In State and
Church we need it, at home and on the
street; in the smallest fashions and in
the most sacred mysteries; that men
should say what they think, should act
out what they believe, should be themselves continually without concealment
and without pretense. When we have

that, then we shall have at least a solid basis of reality on which to build all future progress.   It is the benefit of great and solemn crises that they give us some characters which manifest this simple Truth, that they make it to some extent the character of all the time.

ONE period collects materials, the next period builds the palace.   The long, hard-working winter gathers with infinite toil the conditions of growth, stores them about the dead unanswering seed, then dies like David, and the spring-time, its successor, bright as Solomon in all his glory, comes and finds the preparation made, and, in the sunshine, builds the temple-plant.

You have seen fathers, not cultivated or educated men, who just accepted it as their task to gather the materials of a cultivated and educated life for their children. Not for them to build the gracious beauty or the massive strength of scholarly attainment; but they were content to get everything ready, and then lay the work of construction into their children's hands, in whose fulfilment of their wise ambitions they themselves should live again. And so it is in human history. Age gathers materials for age. One century with slow and painful labor beats out a few crude ideas, which lie like David's logs of wood and blocks of stone and seem merely to cumber the ground. A new century comes, and, inheriting the unfinished plan, it takes these crude ideas, and, lo, they are just what it needs. It finds them hewn to fit each other, and out of them it builds the compact and graceful beauty of its institutions.

TRUTHS are the roots of duties. A rootless duty, one that has no truth below it out of which it grows, has no life, and will have no growth.

MEN talk about morality as one thing, and religion as another. Sometimes they pit them one against the other, as if there were some sort of natural antagonism between the two. We take a higher ground, insisting that there can be no such thing as morality without religion, and that morality becomes more and more genuine just in proportion as religion becomes more and more sound and true. We do not believe in any reform which finds its whole motive within the region of human relations. We look for the permanent success of no effort, however noble its appointed aim may be, which does not draw its impulse from some association of humanity with a power and a will above its own.

WITHOUT settling detailed judgments, which it is not our place to do, we feel sure, in general, that God has bound our whole nature into such a perfect unity that no man can hold wrong opinions without incurring, just so far, danger of injury to his moral life.

ONCE accept this supreme importance of truth, and every part of our nature becomes anxious for the preservation of the testimonies of God. The great doctrines of our faith become the great pillars of our life.

ALL union between such complicated individualities as men involves surrender, the temporary stripping off of non-essentials that the essential may go on and do its work unhindered. Afterward, in the later stages of its labor, each portion of the union may resume its non-essentials, which are not therefore non-importants.

IT is the great boon of such characters as Mr. Lincoln's, that they reunite what

God has joined together and man has put asunder. In him was vindicated the greatness of real goodness and the goodness of real greatness. The twain were one flesh. Not one of all the multitudes who stood and looked up to him for direction with such a loving and implicit trust can tell you to-day whether the wise judgments that he gave came most from a strong head or a sound heart. If you ask them they are puzzled. There are men as good as he, but they do bad things. There are men as intelligent as he, but they do foolish things. In him goodness and intelligence combined and made their best result of wisdom.

THE simple natures and forces will always be the most pliant ones. Water

bends and shapes itself to any new channel.   Air folds and adapts itself to each
new figure.   They are the simplest and
the most infinitely active things in nature.
So this nature, in very virtue of its simplicity, must be also free, always fitting
itself to each new need.   It will always
start from the most fundamental and
eternal conditions, and work in the
straightest even although they be the
newest ways to the present prescribed
purpose.   In one word it must be broad
and independent and radical.

PERFECT truth consists not merely in
the right constituents of character, but
in their right and intimate conjunction.
This union of the mental and moral into

a life of admirable simplicity is what we most admire in children, but in them it is unsettled and unpractical. But when it is preserved into a manhood, deepened into reliability and maturity, it is that glorified childlikeness, that high and reverend simplicity which shames and baffles the most accomplished astuteness, and is chosen by God to fill his purposes when he needs a ruler for his people of faithful and true heart.

IT is inevitable, till man be far more unfeeling and untrue to his convictions than he has always been, that a great wrong asserting itself vehemently should arouse to no less vehement assertion the opposing right.

WHEN shall we learn that with all true men it is not what they intend to do, but it is what the qualities of their natures bind them to do, that determines their career?

WITH a reverent and clear mind to be controlled by events, means to be controlled by God.

TRUTH and justice are in their very nature mighty and intolerant, and must fight with and conquer falsehood and sin in any region of this many-regioned universe where they may meet.

IT is not possible until the need comes, I suppose, that we should feel how legit-

imate and true an accompaniment of
every perfect nature is Force; that is,
the ability to clear its field and do its
work even by the violent destruction of
the hinderances that block its way.

SHALL we say that force, or compul-
sion, is something that is so low that it
can belong to the devil only? that God
can have nothing to do with it, and so
that great truths and causes, high principles, which are the angels of God, his
Michaels, have no right to strive; that
they must not fight with their dragons?
Very important it seems to me that we
should understand the opposite.

THE more we see of events the less we

come to believe in any fate or destiny except the destiny of character.

WE make too little always of the physical. . . . Who shall say that even with David the son of Jesse, there was not a physical as well as a spiritual culture in the struggle with the lion and the bear which occurred among the sheepfolds, out of which God took him to be the ruler of his people?

THERE is a certain wide-spread nervousness and fear of giving force any true place in the world. It seems a horrible intruder, soon, we pray, to be cast out. And yet force is as truly the companion

of reason as body is of spirit. Righteous
force is the reaction of truth upon opposing matter.

THIS great and gracious nature tempts
me with all her alluring motherliness to
bow my will to hers and use her only in
obedience to her own laws. But if I refuse, she flings her tempest at me, or
she sinks my ship, or scorches my un-
shielded head with her fiery suns, or
paralyzes me with disease, and compels
me back into the obedience from which
I foolishly and arrogantly tried to escape.

ANY baby may set his will against the
will of Mother Nature, and refuse to
listen to her reason; but the most colos-

sal giant must yield his actions to her requirements and submit to her majestic force.

I CANNOT draw my picture of the perfect and perfectly effective man or state, unless I lodge the tenderest sympathy and the wisest judgment in a strong, healthy body that shall compel respect and demand obedience when the higher powers fail.

FROM his boyhood up he [Abraham Lincoln] lived in direct and vigorous contact with men and things, not as in older states and easier conditions with words and theories; and both his moral convictions and his intellectual opinions gathered from that contact a supreme degree of that character by which men knew him — that character which is the most distinctive possession of the best American nature—that almost indescribable quality which we call in general clearness or truth, and which appears in the physical structure as health, in the moral constitution as honesty, in the mental structure as sagacity, and in the region of active life as practicalness.

EVERYWHERE this earnestness of desire that truth should work, should move, should go. And what then? Why, of necessity, that if in going it should meet perhaps some obstinate resistance which will not yield, then it must break down. The brute circumstance must not tyrannize over and stop the progress of the spiritual essence.

IN all the simplest characters the line between the mental and moral natures is always vague and indistinct. They run together, and in their best combinations you are unable to discriminate in the wisdom which is their result, how much is moral and how much is intellectual. You are unable to tell whether in the wise acts and words which issue from such a life there is more of the righteousness that comes of a clear conscience or of the sagacity that comes of a clear brain. In more complex characters and under more complex conditions, the moral and the mental lives come to be less healthily combined. They co-operate, they help each other less. They come even to stand over against each other as antagonists; till we have that vague but most melancholy notion which pervades the life of all elaborate civilization, that goodness and greatness, as we call them, are not to be looked for together, till we expect to see and so do see a feeble and narrow conscientiousness on the one hand and a bad unprincipled intelligence on the other, dividing the suffrages of men.

THIS truth comes to us more and more the longer that we live, that on what field or in what uniform, or with what aims we do our duty, matters very little, or even what our duty is, great or small, splendid or obscure. Only to find our duty certainly and somewhere, somehow do it faithfully, makes us good, strong, happy, and useful men, and tunes our lives into some feeble echo of the life of God.